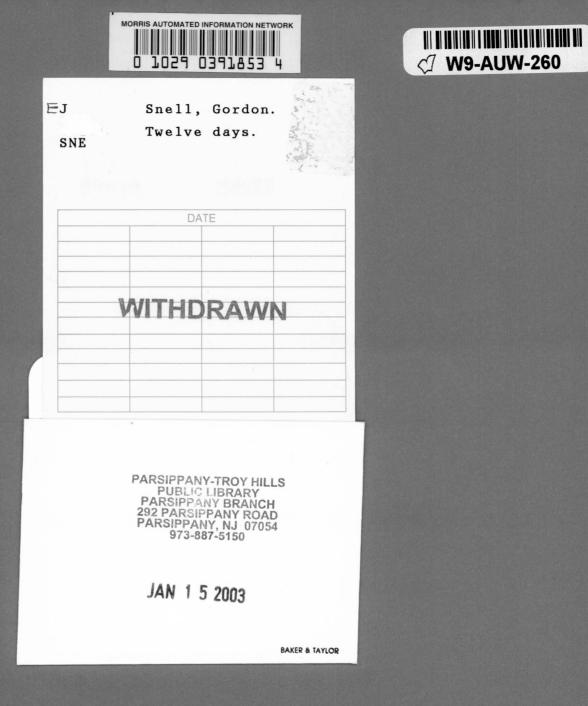

EJ

SNE

Snell, Gordon.
Twelve days.

Twelve Days

A Christmas Countdown

By Gordon Snell

Illustrated by Kevin O'Malley

HarperCollinsPublishers

For dearest Maeve, with all my love
—G.S.

For Dara, my reason for being
—K.O.

Twelve Days: A Christmas Countdown
Text copyright © 2002 by Gordon Snell
Illustrations copyright © 2002 by Kevin O'Malley
Printed in Hong Kong. All rights reserved.
www.harperchildrens.com

Library of Congress Cataloging-in-Publication Data
Snell, Gordon.
Twelve Days: A Christmas Countown / by Gordon Snell ; illustrated by Kevin O'Malley.
p.   cm.
Summary: In this adaptation of the traditional English folk song, "The Twelve Days of Christmas,"
a child's parents provide an increasing number of items to decorate a little pine tree.
ISBN 0-06-028954-6 — ISBN 0-06-028955-4 (lib. bdg.)
1. Children's songs—United States—Texts.   2. Christmas music—Texts.
[1. Christmas music.   2. Songs.]   I. O'Malley, Kevin, 1961– ill.   II. Title.
PZ8.3.S6725 Tw   2002   2001039291
782.42164'0268— dc21   [E]

Typography by Elynn Cohen 1 2 3 4 5 6 7 8 9 10 ❖ First Edition

On the first day of Christmas,
my parents gave to me:
a star-topped little pine tree.

On the second day of Christmas,
my parents gave to me:
two candy canes
to hang on my little pine tree.

On the third day of Christmas,
my parents gave to me:
three nice mice, two candy canes
to hang on my little pine tree.

On the fourth day of Christmas, my parents gave to me:
four teddy bears, three nice mice, two candy canes
to hang on my little pine tree.

On the fifth day of Christmas,
my parents gave to me:
five shining balls, four teddy bears,
three nice mice, two candy canes
to hang on my little pine tree.

On the sixth day of Christmas,
my parents gave to me:
six dancing dollies, five shining balls,
four teddy bears, three nice mice,
two candy canes
to hang on my little pine tree.

On the seventh day of Christmas,
my parents gave to me:
seven singing songbirds, six dancing dollies,
five shining balls, four teddy bears,
three nice mice, two candy canes
to hang on my little pine tree.

On the eighth day of Christmas, my parents gave to me:
eight lights a-winking, seven singing songbirds,
six dancing dollies, five shining balls,
four teddy bears, three nice mice,
two candy canes
to hang on my little pine tree.

On the ninth day of Christmas, my parents gave to me:
nine smiling snowmen, eight lights a-winking,
seven singing songbirds, six dancing dollies,
five shining balls, four teddy bears,
three nice mice, two candy canes
to hang on my little pine tree.

On the tenth day of Christmas, my parents gave to me:
ten red-nosed reindeer,
nine smiling snowmen,
eight lights a-winking,
seven singing songbirds,
six dancing dollies,
five shining balls,

four teddy bears,
three nice mice,
two candy canes
to hang on my
little pine tree.

On the eleventh day of Christmas,
my parents gave to me:
eleven eager elves,
ten red-nosed reindeer,
nine smiling snowmen,
eight lights a-winking,
seven singing songbirds,
six dancing dollies,

five shining balls,
four teddy bears,
three nice mice,
two candy canes
to hang on my
little pine tree.

On the twelfth day of Christmas, my parents gave to me:
twelve Christmas angels, eleven eager elves,
ten red-nosed reindeer, nine smiling snowmen,
eight lights a-winking, seven singing songbirds,
six dancing dollies, five shining balls,
four teddy bears, three nice mice,
two candy canes to hang on my little pine tree.

Early Christmas morning, old Santa
came and said to me . . .